Tim Burton's
The Nightmare Before Christmas

The

Thirteen
Days
of
Christmas

Tim Burton's THE NIGHTMARE BEFORE CHRISTMAS

For information address
Disney Press, 114 Fifth Avenue, New York, New York 10011

10 9 8 7 6 5 4 3 2 1

Library of Congress Cataloging-in-Publication Data on file

Printed in Malaysia

First Printing

Book design by Alfred Giuliani

ISBN 978-1-4231-1804-6

The Thirteen Days of Christmas

By Steven Davison and Carolyn Gardner

Artwork by Tim Wollweber and Sherri Lundberg

Based on a story and characters created by Tim Burton

New York

On the first day of Christmas
my ghoul love gave to me

a star for
my fortune-card tree.

On the second day of Christmas
my ghoul love gave to me

two true-love potions,

and a star for my fortune-card tree.

On the third day of Christmas
my ghoul love gave to me

three lifelines extending,

two true-love potions,

and a star for my fortune-card tree.

On the fourth day of Christmas
my ghoul love gave to me

four wheels of fortune,

three lifelines extending,

two true-love potions,

and a star for my fortune-card tree.

On the fifth day of Christmas

my ghoul love gave to me

five lucky charms!

four wheels of fortune,
three lifelines extending,
two true-love potions,
and a star for my fortune-card tree.

On the sixth day of Christmas
my ghoul love gave to me

six mystic mirrors,

five lucky charms!

four wheels of fortune,
three lifelines extending,
two true-love potions,
and a star for my fortune-card tree.

On the seventh day of Christmas
my ghoul love gave to me

seven pearls of wisdom,

six mystic mirrors,

five lucky charms!

four wheels of fortune,

three lifelines extending,

two true-love potions,

and a star for my fortune-card tree.

On the eighth day of Christmas
my ghoul love gave to me

eight orbs of knowledge,

seven pearls of wisdom,

six mystic mirrors,

five lucky charms!

four wheels of fortune,

three lifelines extending,

two true-love potions,

and a star for my fortune-card tree.

On the ninth day of Christmas
my ghoul love gave to me

nine magic crystals,

eight orbs of knowledge,

seven pearls of wisdom,

six mystic mirrors,

five lucky charms!

four wheels of fortune,

three lifelines extending,

two true-love potions,

and a star for my fortune-card tree.

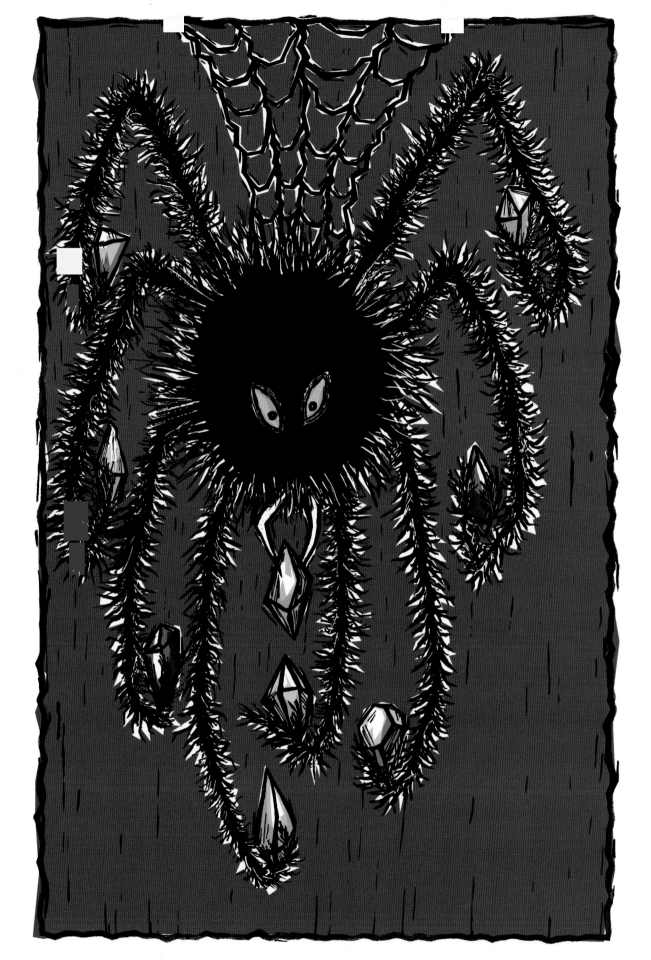

On the tenth day of Christmas
my ghoul love gave to me

ten telling tea leaves,

nine magic crystals,

eight orbs of knowledge,

seven pearls of wisdom,

six mystic mirrors,

five lucky charms!

four wheels of fortune,

three lifelines extending,

two true-love potions,

and a star for my fortune-card tree.

On the eleventh day of Christmas
my ghoul love gave to me

eleven candles floating,

ten telling tea leaves,

nine magic crystals,

eight orbs of knowledge,

seven pearls of wisdom,

six mystic mirrors,

five lucky charms!

four wheels of fortune,

three lifelines extending,

two true-love potions,

and a star for my fortune-card tree.

On the twelfth day of Christmas
my ghoul love gave to me

twelve twinkling star signs,

eleven candles floating,

ten telling tea leaves,

nine magic crystals,

eight orbs of knowledge,

seven pearls of wisdom,

six mystic mirrors,

five lucky charms!

four wheels of fortune,

three lifelines extending,

two true-love potions,

and a star for my fortune-card tree.

On the thirteenth day of Christmas
my ghoul love gave to me

thirteen rings of power,

twelve twinkling star signs,

eleven candles floating,

ten telling tea leaves,

nine magic crystals,

eight orbs of knowledge,

seven pearls of wisdom,

six mystic mirrors,

five lucky charms!

four wheels of fortune,

three lifelines extending,

two true-love potions,